Mind Your Own Business

MIND YOUR OWN BUSINESS

Words by
Michael Rosen

Pictures by
Quentin Blake

André Deutsch

First published 1974 by
André Deutsch Limited
105 Great Russell Street, London WC1

Printed Offset Litho in Great Britain by
Cox & Wyman Limited
London, Fakenham and Reading

ISBN 0 233 96468 1

What's that there?
What's what where?
I want to know what this is
Keep your hair on mate:
'Mind Your Own Business.'

Right now
I'd like best of all not to be here.
I've been thinking that for an hour now.
The trouble is
I don't know where I'd like to be more.
I mean – I like the films –
but that's miles away
I'd be so annoyed when I got there
I wouldn't like it at all
And I'd get even more angry coming back
so I'd hate it even more here –
When I did get back. Hours and hours from now.
So there's no point in making it worse for myself here
and get tired doing it.
Because I'm pretty tired now to tell the truth.
And fancy being even more tired
and coming back to this place
from somewhere that wasn't better
I might be doing quite well really
perhaps it's a lucky streak.
It is a pity the way no one pops in to say hallo.
They know I'm only just round the corner.
All they need do is just – get up and walk round.
So lazy.

I've had this shirt
that's covered in dirt
for years and years and years.

It used to be red
but I wore it in bed
and it went grey
cos I wore it all day
for years and years and years.

The arms fell off
in the Monday wash
and you can see my vest
through the holes in the chest
for years and years and years.

As my shirt falls apart
I'll keep the bits
in a biscuit tin
on the mantelpiece
for years and years and years.

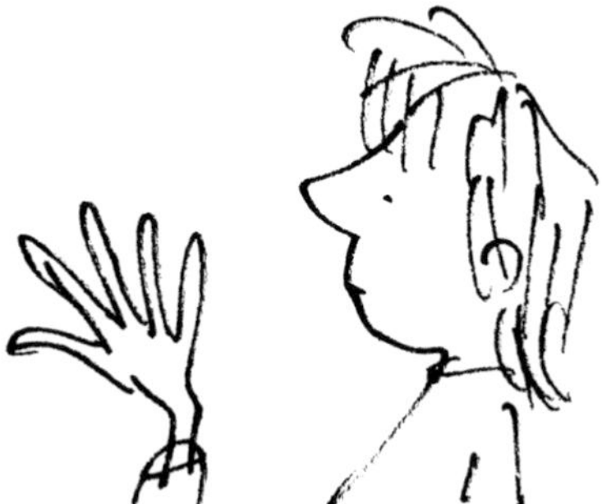

This is the hand
that touched the frost
that froze my tongue
and made it numb

this is the hand
that cracked the nut
that went in my mouth
and never came out

this is the hand
that slid round the bath
to find the soap
that wouldn't float

this is the hand
on the hot water bottle
meant to warm my bed
that got lost instead

this is the hand
that held the bottle
that let go of the soap
that cracked the nut
that touched the frost
this is the hand
that never gets lost.

Saturdays I put on my boots to go wading
down the River Pinn
singing songs like: Olly Jonathan Curly and Carrot
past garden trees, the backs of shops, building sites
scaffolds and timber, park-keepers' huts
the disused railway line and the new estate
the garage junk heap, twenty foot high in greasy
    springs
unstuffed car-seats, boxes in thousands
light bulbs, rubber stamps and an old typewriter,
through the woods where the woodpeckers used
    to be

and there are rapids and bogs and sand-flats,
you have to watch for hidden jaws in the mud
or beaver dams and Amazon settlements;
you can see into the back of the telephone exchange
to a million wires on the walls
and an all-red telephone
and there's Grolly's Grotto:
the tunnel under the library under the cleaners
under the bicycle sheds and the newspaper stand.
In the middle it smells black,
you can't see either end
the walls are wet and the water's deeper
where Thatcher fell in and under
and screamed for hours so it echoed and echoed
but we couldn't see him –
all we could hear was him splashing and thrashing
hitting the walls with his boots
us holding on to the mucky bricks
bumping into each other's arms
or shouting and shushing until it went quiet
and still in the dark. And then we ran.
Or swam. And fought. It was miles.
Rushed into the light covered in slime
looking at each other with eyes big and silly:
Where's Thatcher?
No one said we'd left him. Just us goggling –
waiting for a splosh or scud
It was raining where we stood
goggling in the light under the library where it was
    warm
not knowing that Thatcher was crawling out the
    other end

'If one is one
if two is two
I'm Jack Straw
what are you?'

'Hallo Jack
I'm new,'
I said.

'No no
it's a game –
and you're dead.'

'you mean like:
"*What'll you take
shield or sheaf?
I'll take shield
and you're the chief.*"'

Then the Captain said:
'What does it matter
what Jack Straw's like?
we want to start our game.'

But Weeble and Redd were there:
'It's not "*shield or sheaf*"
it's "*bubble and squeak*" round here.'

'Don't you mean "*puddn and beef*"?'

'You mean he means:
"*Pick me poke me
call me thief.*"'

Then the Captain said:
'What does it matter
what you mean?
I want to start my game.'
He turned and shouted in my face:
'Since you came round this place
nothing's been the same.'

If you don't put your shoes on before I count fifteen
then we won't go to the woods to climb the chestnut
   one
        But I can't find them
Two
        I can't
They're under the sofa three
        No
        O yes
Four five six
        Stop – they've got knots they've got knots
You should untie the laces when you take your shoes
   off seven
        Will you do one shoe while I do the other
        then?
Eight but that would be cheating
        Please
All right
        It always . . .
Nine
        It always sticks – I'll use my teeth

Ten
>
> It won't it won't
> It has – look.

Eleven
>
> I'm not wearing any socks

Twelve
>
> Stop counting stop counting. Mum where
> are my socks mum

They're in your shoes. Where you left them.
>
> I didn't

Thirteen
>
> O they're inside out and upside down and
> bundled up

Fourteen
>
> Have you done the knot on the shoe you
> were . . .

Yes
Put it on the right foot
>
> But socks don't have right and wrong foot

The shoes silly
Fourteen and a half
>
> I am I am. Wait.
> Don't go to the woods without me
> Look that's one shoe already

Fourteen and threequarters
>
> There

You haven't tied the bows yet
>
> We could do them on the way there

No we won't fourteen and seven eights
>
> Help me then
> You know I'm not fast at bows

Fourteen and fifteen sixteeeenths
>
> A single bow is all right isn't it

Fifteen we're off
>
> See I did it.
> Didn't I?

Every few weeks someone looks at me and says:
my you've grown
and then every few weeks someone says:
they've grown too long

and silver scissors come out of the drawer
and chip at my toes and run through my hair.

Now I don't like this one little bit
I won't grow if I'm going to be chopped
what's me is mine and I want to keep it
so either the scissors or my nails had better stop.

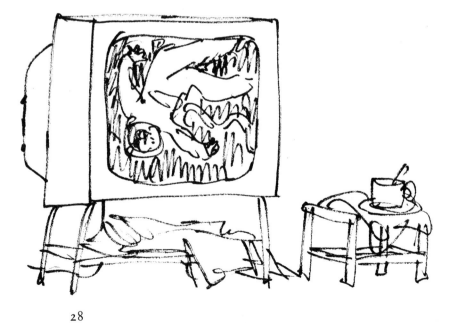

```
          5
          4
          3
          2
          1 rocket
          2 the moon
          3 flew it
what 4?
          5
          4
          3
          2
          1 rocket
```

My dad's thumb
can stick pins in wood
without flinching –
it can crush family-size matchboxes
in one stroke
and lever off jam-jar lids without piercing
at the pierce here sign.

If it wanted
it could be a bath-plug
or a paint-scraper
a keyhole cover or a tap-tightener.

It's already a great nutcracker
and if it dressed up
it could easily pass
as a broad bean or a big toe.

In actual fact, it's quite simply
the world's fastest envelope burster.

This morning my father looks out the window, rubs
  his nose
and says: Lets go and saw up logs
me and you.
So I put on my thick blue socks
and he puts on his army vest
and he keeps saying: Are you ready are you ready
It's a snorter of a day just look at the trees
and I run downstairs to get my old bent boots
that everybody says go round corners on their own
  they're so bent
and he comes in saying that his tobacco is like old
  straw
which means that he is going to smoke his pipe today
So he says to mum: We'll be back in an hour or two
which means not for ages
but mum doesn't hear, because we lumberjacks are
  out the door in a flash

I said:
I'll tell you what I did in town
I saw a greengrocer in the underground
with his pockets full of oranges,
a paperboy yawned
so you could see his tonsils,
there was one old football boot
lying in city square
and round the island came the Odeon commissionaire
riding on a moped with his uniform flying,
a hamster saw a parrot sneeze
the shop blinds flapped and an oiltanker squealed,
the peanut man
lost a bag beneath a bus's wheels
'Mind your peanuts' a girl shouted
his tray was slipping and a taxi hooted
'O help me then' he called out
I said: 'where I'm sorry where'
and forty thousand pigeons climbed into the air.

Down behind the dustbin
I met a dog called Jim.
He didn't know me
and I didn't know him.

I'm a man.
    A grown up man?
A nearly man.
    A man in short trousers?
Short trouser man.
    Can you drive?
I walk to the park.
    A short trouser park keeper?
I'm a goalie.
    And can't touch the bar?
But I'm growing.
    Growing?
Bit by bit.
    A bit on the top?
To reach the bar.
    And a bit on the bottom?
To lengthen into longs.
    And then you'll be a bit of a park-keeper?
No. Then I'll be goalie.
    In long trousers?
No. In shorts.
    I don't see the point.
Who asked you to?

39

This ship in the dock was at the end of its trip
The man on deck was the captain of the ship
The name of the captain was Old Ben Brown
He played the ukelele with his trousers down.

Some called him Rover
Some called him Mog
Some called him dog-cat
Some the cat-dog

They gave him a kennel
He slept on the roof
Bow-miaow he growled
Grrr-purr, purr-woof

He wagged his tail
Up a tree he flew
He found a mouse to tease
and a bone to chew

Strangers at the door
made him bark
His eyes went green
and shone in the dark

Tom cats chased him
Alsatian dogs bit him
A kitten wouldn't play
and two boys hit him.

Off he ran
up yonders lane
and no one ever
saw him again.

It was spring in the fields and woods
the leaves in the hedges shook in the wind
as a crow stood quite still on a white horse's back.
He was looking at the grass about him
and the trees at the edge of the paddock
when all of a sudden he said to the horse beneath his
  feet:
Do you see how green everything is today?
and the horse said:
well to tell you the truth – no, I don't.
everything looks pink to me
you see my eyes are pink . . . he stopped.
the crow spoke again:
Oh. I'm sorry.
But how do you know that everything you see is pink
when it's the only colour you've ever seen?
The horse sat thinking about that for a while
and then said:
well of course it's quite true what you say.
In fact I was only guessing.
But you see – when I was born,
everybody pointed at me and said: look at him –
his eyes are pink. So I thought everything I saw
was pink. It seemed a sensible thing to do at the time.
The crow shook his head slowly to and fro
breathed in deeply and sympathetically
and flew off to make his nest in the clear green sky.

45

My brother got married in a wimpy bar
just round the corner – it isn't far
and not dirty or cheap. They've done it up nice.
Of course you have to pay – but it's worth the price:
three and nine for a brunchberger and a couple of
    cokes.
I like the cheese and egg special – but not the folks.
Whatever it is, they have to have chips and a cup of
    tea
finish with a bun, pop out for a pee
carry on with beer perhaps – but anyway:
there's Mike and Sally – O I didn't say
Sally's Mike's wife and Mike's my brother.
Sally's dad didn't come and Mrs Beaumont's her
    mother.
So there's Mike and Sally – they'd done the marrying
    bit
– only the Town Hall – but you still have to wear the
    kit:
dad in a hat, me with a flower.
'Only', I said? – it cost – well I wasn't told, but it
    lasted an hour
and the man who did it was fantastically clean.

He hides behind a door where he can't be seen
when in he creeps with his black silk tie on
as if they're the first couple he ever set eye on.
I had the ring being best – or as Mike says – worst
    man.

I was as well – worst I mean.

The night before I had an omelette –
needed something to spice it,
found an old tube of something called Patsy's Garlic
    Paste
squeezed the lot on. (It said: Add to taste)
But maybe I'm a quicker adder than taster
(add first, taste later)
but I might just as well have skipped the eggs
– my mouth came up red. I felt shaky round the legs,
started sweating, I couldn't keep my hands still.
But it wasn't so much me – It was the smell:
the kitchen, the bathroom, the garden shed,
the stairs, the landing, and then in bed.

Sunk under the pillow, thrashed the blankets to a
    heap

– I thought maybe I'd lose it with sleep.
For a start I couldn't shut my eyes – but in the
    morning
I was woken up with a kind of – well – something
    roaring.
I thought maybe it had reached my ears
but two seconds later it said: 'Not in twenty years –
the Normandy Landings – that was the last time'
and in rushed dad: 'O this is fine bloody fine.
It's like a Paris sewer in here.'
Mum's saying: 'What is it? What is it?' – 'Beer'
says Mike. But dad knew:
'Go on. Tell them. You.'

I said I was sorry and that I'd felt a bit hungry
and I hoped they wouldn't get too angry
it being a special day and everything.
'Best man. The one who hands me the damn ring. –
Just don't breathe when you hand it me.' Mike says
and poor old mum just stood there with tears in her
    eyes.

48

'What about Mrs Beaumont?' 'Half an hour to go.'
'Where's my collar?' 'It's all right – it won't show.'
'What? The collar?' 'No. The smell.'
'We've run out of soap.' 'Like hell.'
'Buy him some tablets. Or a mouth spray.'
'I've found the collar but no stud.' 'What a day. What
   a day.'

We went to the Town Hall via the chemist and tailor:
Mike holding my mouth and me his collar.
Soon the whole car smelt of peppermint cream.
'Never again. What a day for the idiot to choose.' 'I
   shall scream.'
But we got there all right, without that much panic
except that Mrs Beaumont met us with: 'Hallo Mike –
   you smell of garlic –
straighten your collar. Sally's here already.
Got the flowers? Don't worry. Take it steady.'

We were inside the Wimpy Bar in two hours –
I didn't say – the manager's a relation of ours.
Shut the doors at one o'clock – let us eat till half past
as many wimpy's as we liked (the ketchup didn't last)

free squash, free tastee-freez.
'But no songs, no dancing please –
the club downstairs are very particular.'
There was no time for dad's one about the blue cater-
    pillar
and there wasn't much fun later really.
Mike ruined the lot. Or nearly.

You see he got up and said:
he was blowed if he was going to run his life like us.
He'd had enough of the area, the people, the working
    class
the middle class, the upper class and all women.
He hated animals, bungalows, me and bed-linen
and the only hope for all of us was love
which none of us had nor never would have.
– Everyone started shouting at each other.
Someone rushed over to Sally's mother.
'And another thing,' says Mike.
'Sally's pregnant. All right?'

I don't really remember what then happened,
I was supposed to have spoken second

(I had it all learnt off: Lovely meal . . . The Happy
   Couple . . .
. . . a quick song . . . aren't they lucky . . . so many
   people.)

But as mum was crying again and Mrs Beaumont had –
– well no one knew what Mrs Beaumont did:
she ran out the door too quick
'Whipped out to have a fit'
and that was that. Mike all smiles
Sally giggling in the corner all the whiles
with dad winking at Mike and consoling mum:
'There there dear. He's just a bit tight' 'Oooh no. Oh
   what's to be done?'

Three hours later when there was just us sitting in
   the front room.
Everyone had gone. It was all quiet at home –
mum suddenly looked up from her knitting and
   shouted:
'I know what. It was the garlic that did it.'

It was a stormy night
one Christmas day
as they fell awake
on the Santa Fe

Turkey, jelly
and the ship's old cook
all jumped out
of a recipe book

The jelly wobbled
the turkey gobbled
and after them both
the old cook hobbled

Gobbler gobbled
Hobbler's Wobbler.
Hobbler gobbled
Wobbler's Gobbler.

Gobbly-gobbler
gobbled Wobbly
Hobbly-hobbler
Gobbled Gobbly.

Gobble gobbled
Hobble's Wobble
Hobble gobbled
gobbled Wobble.

gobble gobble
wobble wobble
hobble gobble
wobble gobble

54

From the winter wind
a cold fly
came to our window
where we had frozen our noses
and warmed his feet on the glass

A spider doesn't fly
but walks off the edge of a beam
and waits for a bump
where all eight feet will feel firm dirt again
and all that silk slack between
will float off till it meets with
the last flakes off the last specks
spinning through the blue.

Wood pigeon
makes a black arrow on the cloud
and a procession between the wheat.
Beats the leaves
of the trees it leaves,
crosses the sun
and gargles in a hedge.

The pigeons in town
race in laps round the ABC cinema
swell on swiss-rolls
and go about in gangs
robbing sparrows.

Joe one struts down our gutter
every morning
and just beneath the window –
gargles.

Anyone would think it was a hedge.

There's a thin man
with a red jacket
lips like bacon rind
walks and whistles
his head knocked left
carries old paper
that crackles in his pocket
buys eucalyptus lozenges
and lives
in a room in a road by a pond
says cheer up bubbles
if we pass on the pavement
and up go his eyebrows
like broken string
his feet are cold
and his children have children now
he says
like me one day soon
and nods some more

Down the road
we see behind wet windows
eyes up
trying to pull the clouds apart.
Before they come out again
they want to see dry islands on the paving-stones
and the drips from the bricks go warm.

We're listening to Niagara in the drains
and camping in Cape Horn under the butcher's
    awning.
We change guard at the tobacconist
watch petrol rainbows in the gutter.
A dog droops there
wishing he had a sou'wester on;
and like our ball hitting the chicken-wire
as he shudders his body
he makes a show of his own rain too.

I saw a lady with red hair
talking to one with blue on

the sun shone
and the rain ran
the streets emptied
the people had gone

when I looked
for the ladies again
there was a purple stream
flowing down the drain

Who rolled in the mud
behind the garage door?
Who left footprints
across the kitchen floor?

I know a dog whose nose is cold
I know a dog whose nose is cold

Who chased raindrops
down the windows?
Who smudged the glass
with the end of his nose?

I know a dog with a cold in his nose
I know a dog with a cold in his nose

Who wants a bath
and a tuppenny ha'penny biscuit?
Who wants to bed down
in his fireside basket?

Me, said Ranzo
I'm the dog with a cold.

In the daytime I am Rob Roy and a tiger
In the daytime I am Marco Polo
                I chase bears in Bricket Wood
In the daytime I am the Tower of London
                nothing gets past me
                when it's my turn
                in Harrybo's hedge
In the daytime I am Henry the fifth and Ulysses
                and I tell stories
                that go on for a whole week
                if I want.
At night in the dark
                when I've shut the front room door
                I try and
                get up the stairs across the landing
                into bed and under the pillow
                without breathing once.

I share my bedroom with my brother
and I don't like it.
His bed's by the window
under my map of England's railways
that has a hole in just above Leicester
where Tony Sanders, he says,
killed a Roman centurion
with the Radio Times.

My bed's in the corner
and the paint on the skirting board
wrinkles when I push it with my thumb
which I do sometimes when I go to bed
sometimes when I wake up
but mostly on Sundays
when we stay in bed all morning.

That's when he makes pillow dens
under the blankets
so that only his left eye shows
and when I go deep-bed mining
for elastoplast spools
that I scatter with my feet
the night before,
and I jump on to his bed
shouting: eeyoueeyoueeyouee
heaping pillows on his head:
'Now breathe, now breathe'
and then there's quiet and silence
so I pull it away quick
and he's there laughing all over
sucking fresh air along his breathing-tube fingers.

Actually, sharing's all right.

Late last night
I lay in bed
driving buses
in my head.

I'm the big sleeper
rolled up in his sheets
at the break of day

I'm a big sleeper living soft
in a hard kind of way

the light through the curtain
can't wake me
I'm under the blankets
you can't shake me
the pillow rustler
and blanket gambler
a mean tough eiderdown man

I keep my head
I stay in bed

Father says
Never
let
me
see
you
doing
that
again
father says
tell you once
tell you a thousand times
come hell or high water
his finger drills my shoulder
never let me see you doing that again

My brother knows all his phrases off by heart
so we practise them in bed at night.

Mum'll be coming home today.
It's three weeks she's been away.
When dad's alone
all we eat
is cold meat
which I don't like
and he burns the toast I want just-brown
and I hate taking the ash-can down.

He's mended the door
from the little fight
on Thursday night
so it doesn't show
and can we have grilled tomatoes
Spanish onions and roast potatoes
and will you sing me 'I'll never more roam'
when I'm in bed, when you've come home.

My brother is making a protest about bread.
'Why do we always have wholemeal bread?
You can't spread butter on wholemeal bread
You try and spread the butter on
and it just makes a hole right through the middle.'

He marches out of the room and shouts
across the landing and down the passage.
'It's always the same in this place.
Nothing works.
The volume knob's broken on the radio you know
It's been broken for months and months you know.'

He stamps back into the kitchen
stares at the loaf of bread and says:
'Wholemeal bread – look at it, look at it.
You put the butter on
and it all rolls up.
you put the butter on
and it all rolls up.'

We were making scrambled eggs yesterday
and mum told my brother not to use a fork
as it's a non-stick frying-pan,
and he said: I know I know I know
I was the one who put you on to these
non-stick frying pans you know.
Today he told me that he was the one
who put mum on to non-stick frying pans.
Everyone interrupts in this house, he says
and he sits in the corner making sheep noises.

you say: let me have your nose
    I would like to use it today
and I say: but it's the only one I've got
    you can't take my nose away

I say: where will you put it?
In my ear, you say
My nose wouldn't fit
you couldn't hear, I say

But you look me in the eye
and say: I've got a secret:
piddle shlops ndeely blins
klip fadaddle splee tit

so next time you're asked
at one of those Trick Mick Shows
'What did the ear 'ear?'
say – 'Only the nose knows.'

peas for breakfast please he said
and a plateful of peas is what he got

and when he went to bed last night
I heard him say: more peas please

you know, I don't think he eats much else
one full bowl three times a day

it would fill a room all those peas you know
but I think
even if he had to wade up to his knees in peas
he would still come here saying: more peas please

'Teasing-toads are never alone
they never hunt in ones
They chase men and women
and drive children mad.
Listen to them boasting –
the teasing toads.'

'I hate your laces
I undo them'
'I love your buttons
I eat them.'

'I am soap-sting
I get in your eye
and make you cry.'

'I'm the one
who burns your tongue'
'I get up your nose
and make it run.'

'I am boot-bug, living in your boots
when you tug – I tug
I don't let go.'

'And when at night
into bed you creep
I'll be there to ruck your sheets.'

'Soap-stings, boot-bugs
long-distance nose runners are we.
Every way, any time,
we tease, we tease.'

85

Hog-pig waits on a mountain
   above a valley in the spring.
Hog-pig waits on a mountain
   above the valley where he is king.

He could – if he would
   chew up churches and trees
   ram his tusks through castle walls
   and bite through men-in-armour
   like a dog cracking fleas

Hog-pig could trumpet in the air
   and make the valleys roar
or wait up on the mountain
   as he's always done before.

Have you seen the Hidebehind?
I don't think you will, mind you,
because as you're running through the dark
the Hidebehind's behind you.

The Sleepy Baby-sitter's Curse

Oh naked bone shine
faff and pander
go to dead –
thistle stalk linen legs.
Why o why
will he never go through bed?

Rustle Me Lamkin
O creep, O crawl, O pillow fall
wind it, bind it
wrap it, mind it
why o why o why
won't he grow.

Nows the wrestle now
one last rattlescome
sting it antwerp
sting it coxcomb
I'll zero. I'm warning. I'll zero
H.Q. – O.K. Zero and out.
Thanks H.Q.

Goodnightgoodnightgoodnightgoodnight.

Sometimes it's night
and too late for you
from the warehouses, stations, schools and yards.
The streets have queues of dead cars.
You're all at home breathing.
Thousands side by side in the terraces
or stacked in flats like a pile of coats.
Your breath gathers round your buildings
and lorries pass sometimes.

High up from mountains
we can see it.
And closer to, we can hear too.

Some say you're resting from the day
we say you're waiting for it.

If I were walking along the canal
I would look in at me reading by the window
and think – I wish I was reading
by that window overlooking the canal
instead of walking along here by the canal
in the rain
and I would look in at all the other windows
and see the pictures on their walls
and the televisions they talk to
and perhaps even the different kinds of tea
moving from hand to hand
each in his own kind of room
and I would feel the damp
rise from the green leaves
where it had just sunk
and all along the walls
the leaves would die an inch more tonight
if I were walking there
looking in at me.

When we opened the door late
to see what had happened to the sky
there were two cats
crouching among the snowdunes
pretending they were fireside laps.
The beads in their eyes stole some of
our kitchen light
and spilt it on to the path.
So we put down the bones of a chop there too
saying: there's some marrow inside that you know –
but they didn't believe it was for them
and sat still thawing their patches
like two warm loaves
and groaning that we hadn't put it near enough
seeing that they had put their feet to bed by now.

I'm alone in the evening
when the family sits
reading and sleeping
and I watch the fire in close
to see flame goblins
wriggling out of their caves
for the evening

Later I'm alone
when the bath has gone cold around me
and I have put my foot
beneath the cold tap
where it can dribble
through valleys between my toes
out across the white plain of my foot
and bibble bibble into the sea

I'm alone
when mum's switched out the light
my head against the pillow
listening to ca thump ca thump
in the middle of my ears.
It's my heart.